I0876015

THE HAUNTED BOOKSHELF

The telling or reading of ghost stories during long, dark, and cold Christmas nights is a yuletide ritual dating back to at least the eighteenth century, and was once as much a part of Christmas tradition as decorating fir trees, feasting on goose, and the singing of carols. During the Victorian era many magazines printed ghost stories specifically for the Christmas season. These "winter tales" didn't necessarily explore Christmas themes. Rather, they were offered as an eerie pleasure to be enjoyed on Christmas Eve with the family, adding a supernatural shiver to the seasonal chill.

The tradition remained strong in the British Isles (and her colonies) throughout much of the twentieth century, though in recent years it has been on the wane. Certainly, few people in Canada or the United States seem to know about it any longer. This series of small books seeks to rectify this, to revive a charming custom for the long, dark nights we all know so well here at Christmastime.

THE HAUNTED BOOKSHELF

Charles Dickens
The Signalman

A.M. Burrage
One Who Saw

Edith Wharton
Afterward

M.R. James
The Diary of Mr. Poynter

Marjorie Bowen
The Crown Derby Plate

E.F. Benson
How Fear Departed the Long Gallery

W.W. Jacobs
The Toll House

Algernon Blackwood
The Empty House

H. Russell Wakefield
The Red Lodge

Frank Cowper
Christmas Eve on a Haunted Hulk

R.H. Malden
The Sundial

Elizabeth Gaskell
The Old Nurse's Story

Daphne du Maurier
The Apple Tree

Richard Bridgeman
The Morgan Trust

M.R. James
The Story of a Disappearance and an Appearance

Walter de la Mare
The Green Room

Margaret Oliphant
The Open Door

THE HAUNTED BOOKSHELF

Bernard Capes
An Eddy on the Floor

F. Marion Crawford
The Doll's Ghost

Edith Wharton
Mr. Jones

Shirley Jackson
A Visit

Cynthia Asquith
The Corner Shop

Gertrude Atherton
The Dead and the Countess

Arthur Conan Doyle
The Captain of the Polestar

Marjorie Bowen
The House by the Poppy Field

Andrew Caldecott
A Room in a Rectory

L.P. Hartley
Podolo

Laurence Whistler
Captain Dalgety Returns

Mary Fitt
The Amethyst Cross

Rosemary Timperley
The Mistress in Black

Sarah Orne Jewett
Lady Ferry

H. Russell Wakefield
Lucky's Grove

Edith Wharton
The Duchess at Prayer

Hugh Walpole
The Little Ghost

Louisa Baldwin
The Weird of the Walfords

THE WEIRD OF THE WALFORDS

BELOVED
WIFE
BELOVED
CHILD

THE WEIRD OF THE WALFORDS

LOUISA BALDWIN

A GHOST STORY FOR CHRISTMAS

DESIGNED & DECORATED BY SETH

BIBLIOASIS

ON A SUMMER'S day in the year 1860, I, Humphrey Walford, did a deed for which I should have been disinherited by my father and disowned by my ancestors. I laid sacrilegious hands on the old carved oak four-post family bedstead and destroyed it.

Alone I could not have accomplished the work of destruction. The massive posts, canopy, and panels would have resisted my single efforts; but I compelled two reluctant men to lend me their aid, and by the help of saws and hatchets we reduced the whole structure to billets of wood such as one might kindle a cheerful flame within the parlour grate on a damp summer evening,

It was a bed with a history to me so unspeakably melancholy that I had resolved when I was my own master I would destroy the gloomy structure, and rid me of the nightmare-like feeling with which the sight of it never failed to inspire me.

The bed itself was upwards of three hundred years old, carved in oak grown on our land, while the heavy, dark green hangings, faded and musty-smelling, dated only from the time of my great-grandfather Walford. I have the dimensions of the huge hearse-like thing by bearer. It was ten feet long by eight feet wide, and ten feet high; and when as a small child I was brought to see my young mother die in the recesses of the vast bed, I looked up at its tall posts with something of the awe with which I should now regard the loftiest tree.

For three centuries this bed had been the cradle and grave of our family. Its heavy drapery had deadened the sound of the first cry and the last groan of the generations of Walfords who had been born or died in Walford Grange. In its solemn depths the newly-wedded brides of the family lay the first few nights in their new home, till the wedding festivities were ended, and the squire and his wife began their everyday married life by occupying a less stately but more comfortable bed. I knew the history of the gloomy old piece of furniture as family tradition had preserved it for three centuries. Ten Squire Walfords had either died in that bed or had lain on it after death awaiting their burial. I was the eleventh squire dating from the epoch of the bed, and I would neither die in it nor be laid upon it after my death. And to make sure of this there was no way but now, in my youth and strength, to full upon it with hatchet and saw and utterly destroy it.

I did not fear death more than my forefathers, but I resented being bidden by family tradition and custom to die in a given spot. I rebelled at having a definite place assigned to me to lie down in and die—a place so fraught with dismal associations as the ancient, hearse-like bed. I could not endure to think that, wander wide as I would, I must return to this bed of death at lost, and here, among stifling pillows and heavy curtains, end my life precisely where it began.

Must this ghastly horror of my childhood be the goal towards which I tend? When I am sailing on mid-ocean, the ship ploughing her way through the furrows of the sea, shall I only be speeding, sooner or later, towards this dismal bed? When I climb mountains and breathe the keen air of the heights, is it but to end in the exclusion of light and air? Must every step I take, every journey I make, be but a stage on the road that ends in the stifling pillows of this bed of death? No, a thousand times no, and I brought my axe down on the footboard with a crash.

How vividly both the dead and living who had occupied this ancient bed rose before my mind's eye! Here had lain Ralph Walford, killed in the Civil Wars, fighting for the king, and his wounded body was brought home and stretched on what had been his bridal bed to await his burial. And here died Squire Ralph's young widow, who, a short time after her husband's sad homecoming, gave birth to his posthumous child, and never again left this ill-omened bed till they carried her out feet foremost. Ralph Walford's brother Heneage, the next squire, thought to make the old bed festive with gold and crimson hangings, to forget that his brother's corpse had lain on it, his orphan child been born in it, and his widow died in it, and by the upholsterer's wit to convert a hearse into a bridal bower.

Brighter times came to our family with the Restoration. We had spent our blood and treasure in the king's cause, for which he did not suffer us to go unhonoured; for shortly after his joyful restoration his gracious majesty was travelling within ten miles of Walford Grange, and, the weather proving stormy, and there being no other Royalist house of consideration near, he made shift to pass a night under the roof of his faithful servant Heneage Walford.

My father often told me the history of that memorable visit, as it had been handed down from generation to generation. How gracious and witty was the king's majesty, how merry and light-hearted, as little troubled by the murder of his royal father and the heavy misfortunes of his house as by the brave lives lost and families impoverished in his cause!

Squire Heneage was as loyal a man as ever drew sword for the king, yet he was heard to say that it was a cursed day for him when his gracious majesty honoured him by being his guest, for it turned his wife Mistress Johanna's head, and she was never again the woman she had been. She grumbled and bemoaned herself that the king had not knighted her husband, so that she might have ruffled it a step above the squirearchy. But one abiding comfort remained with her from the royal visit. And this was that both at coming and going the king had saluted her, and she ever after prettily described the royal manner of kissing, which she affirmed to differ from that practised by ordinary men. Mistress Johanna's serving woman, Anne Grimshaw, said that the king had saluted her too; but this her mistress would not hear of, and when she appealed to Squire Heneage he set the vexed question at rest by giving his opinion that, judging it as a matter of probability, it was more likely that a vain woman should lie, than that his sacred majesty should kiss Anne Grimshaw, who had a foul face of her own.

If I have somewhat enlarged on the fact of the king's visit to Walford Grange, it is not so much on account of any tokens of his royal favour that be was pleased to bestow on my ancestors, as because he lay in the bedchamber, in the great oak bed with its brave new hangings. But the king was tormented by terrible dreams, and woke in the morning haggard and weary, as though he had been ridden by witches. And that I attributed to a malign influence in the hearse-like bed itself, and with that I crashed into it afresh.

I had long promised myself this fierce destructive joy, when I in my turn should be master of Walford Grange. My father had died in this bed three years ago, and I had been travelling in the south of Europe ever since, urged partly by the restless curiosity of youth, and partly by the belief that no Squire Walford had ever crossed the seas before. Some younger sons and thriftless members of our family, in pursuit of the fortune denied them at home, had ventured into foreign lands, but the head of the house never. My father met any wishes or arguments I advanced on the subject of travel by a statement that seemed to him conclusive—that a man sees enough in his own country that he can't understand, without going abroad

to complete his confusion. But now on my return home I hastened to carry out my design on the hated ancestral bed.

What consternation prevailed in the house when it was understood what I was about, and when I and Gillam the carpenter and his man, having stripped the great bed of its drapery, proceeded to take to pieces the panels of the carved oak canopy! Mrs Barrett, the old housekeeper, stood wiping her honest eyes and bewailing my impiety.

"Don't 'ee do it, squire, don't 'ee do it! You may come to know the want of a good feather bed to die in yet! Such a bed as it's been for lyings in and layings out, and I'd hoped to ha' seen you laid in it, like your poor father before you."

What Mrs Barrett's expectation of life may have been I know not, but she was sixty-five, and I twenty-four years of age.

"My good Barrett, I have determined that this bed shall utterly perish. We will not contribute one more corpse to its greedy maw. But if it be its feathers that you bewail, you are welcome to its pillows to line your nest with, but the bed itself must perish.'

"What, squire, the bed that your great uncle Geoffrey was found dead in, when he'd gone upstairs overnight as well and as hearty as ever man was, and making his ungodly jokes, the Lord forgive him! The very bed as your grandfather lay in two whole years before he died, and all the house heard his groans; and where your Aunt Hester was laid with the water drip, drip from every limb, just as they brought her in drowned from the brook!"

"Yes, my good Barrett, because of these very things the bed must perish."

Then Gillam began, as he took off his paper cap and wiped his brow: "If it's as the bed don't seem natural like to sleep in after so many o' your kin has laid stiff and stark in it, won't you sell it, squire, to them as knows nothing of its ways? That there panel with the berried ivy on it is a deal too pretty a bit of carving to make firewood on."

"No, Gillam, I shall not sell it. The man who would take money for the bed his ancestors died in, would sell their bones to make knife-handles of. Besides, the bed has existed long enough; it has served my family to die in for ten generations. It's my own property, Gillam; mayn't I do what I will with my own?"

"Ay, surely, squire; there's no law to hinder a man making any fool of hisself as he pleases wi' what's his own. But I sides with the chap as made the bedstead, and I shouldn't like to think as in a matter o' two or three hundred years a bit o' my work 'ud be chopped up for firing."

"Be under no uneasiness, Gillam; you and I do not live in an age that produces lasting work. Our glue-and-tintack carpentry is not done with a view to posterity."

"Well, squire," continued Gillam, returning to his first idea, "if you won't sell the bedstead whole nor piecemeal, you might give me them panels with the carved ivy on 'em. I could find you some bits o' wood as 'ud burn brighter and better."

"I don't mind giving you the old ivy carving, Gillam," I said, "but only on condition that I shall never see anything more of it, in any shape or form."

"That's easy promised, sir, and thank you kindly. I'll make it up into something as'll surprise itself."

Having weakly consented to his request, I saw him lay aside two or three beautiful panels, richly carved with branches of berried ivy, as salvage from the general wreck.

If the gloomy horrors of the old bed had not eaten into my very heart, I could never have lent a hand at such a work of destruction. I should at least have saved the footboard with its carving in high relief of Adam and Eve under the tree, a man-headed serpent twining round the trunk, and the branches bending beneath their load of fruit. But I could not look at it without thinking of the dying eyes that had fixed their fading gaze on it, so my axe and saw made havoc of a work of art. When the floor was littered over with billets of wood, and the men were wiping their hot faces, I felt a strange lightness of heart, a comfortable sense of work postponed at length happily accomplished.

"Gillam," I said, "there was timber enough in that huge thing to build a man-of-war, drapery to make her sails, and rope enough for all her rigging."

"Ay, there was a'most;" and, hastily throwing his tools into his basket, he added, sarcastically I thought, "There'll be nothing else I can help you to pull down or to smash up, squire?"

I soon found that my destructive toil had benefited me in more ways than one. Not only had it freed me from an intolerable oppression of spirit, but it had established for me in the neighbourhood a reputation for eccentricity, which I maintained afterwards at the smallest cost, and found of great service. The carrying out of my long-cherished purpose was regarded as evidence of a wild and lawless disposition, bordering on mental derangement. Night after night at the alehouse Gillam recounted to a breathless audience the story of the scene of destruction at which he had assisted professionally. And it grew in the telling till, without the slightest intention of lying, he added that the squire's rage against the old place was such, that he had been obliged to menace him with the screwdriver to keep him from tearing down the mantelshelf and wainscot.

I was evidently a man whom it was not wise to thwart or contradict. My servants flew at my least word with an alacrity I had not before observed. My bidding was promptly done, my orders were not disputed, and whatever I said was agreed to with servility. While enjoying the sweets of mental health, as my neighbours voted me on such insufficient grounds on the borderland of insanity, I availed myself of the liberty it gave me to speak and act as I chose. Their hasty judgement had made me free of the wide domain of conduct. There was nothing I could do, however extravagant, but was clearly shadowed forth in the destruction of the ancestral oak bed.

I began to grow lonely in Walford Grange. My good Barrett died suddenly, and in my solitude I wanted someone to sit and talk with me in the long evenings, for even the bright wood fire flickering on the hearth could not satisfy all my desires for cheerful companionship. I should not have wished to marry if I had had a brother to live with me, to share my thoughts and occupations, and who would himself marry and preserve the name. But I was the last of the family, and I did not mean to let an ancient race die out.

I began seriously to think of marrying, though whom, I had not an idea, for so far I had not seen the woman I should care to marry, nor could I suppose that anyone looked with an eye of favour upon me. But when a man makes up his mind to marry, and sets out on his travels by land and sea, resolved never to return to his home till he brings a wife with him, it would be hard if he could not effect his purpose.

It happened that I met with my wife unexpectedly, and where I should have thought I was least likely to meet her—in a log house in the far west of America. Her name was Grace Calvert, and she was only eighteen years old, fair and fresh as an unfolding flower, and full of the high spirits and delight of life suited to her age and her free and simple bringing up. I fell in love with her at first sight, and we were married after a short courtship, for I had obtained the object of my travel, and my little wife was wild with curiosity and impatience to see England. She had a most romantic conception of the land of her forefathers, and delighted me by her belief that every village in England contained a church, vast and venerable as Westminster Abbey, and was engirt with hills crowned by frowning fortresses.

Grace had never seen houses built either of brick or stone, and had I not been able to show her a photograph of Walford Grange, it would have been impossible to give her any idea of an object so strange that there was nothing within the narrow limits of her experience with which to compare it. Her imagination was greatly stirred by the picture of the old house. Not a detail escaped her, from the fluted chimneys to the stone seats in the wide porch. The oriel windows, with their diamond panes, pleased my young wife more than anything, and especially she admired the broad windows of the best bedchamber, in which some two years before I had wrought my destructive will on the ancestral bed. The room was now bare and stripped of furniture, and since Mrs Barrett's death I had kept it constantly locked.

Grace was fascinated with the position of the room, with its large window over the porch, looking down the avenue of limes by which the house was approached, to the open country, and the line of low hills that bounded the horizon.

"That room must be lighter than those on the ground floor," she said. "See how the upper storey projects and throws a shadow over the lower rooms? We will make it our sitting room, will we not?"

The request gave me a strange sinking of heart, and I felt that not even the society of my young wife could induce me to live in the room that had so long contained the hearse-like bed. I temporised with her in a vague manner, neither granting nor denying her request. I begged her to wait till she could see for herself how much better adapted to the comfort of daily life were the rooms on the ground floor than those on the upper storey.

In all her short life, Grace had not been further than twenty miles from the spot where she was born, and I feared lest taking her away from all she loved, and from everything with which she was familiar, might prove too keen a pain.

There was a brief tempest of tears at parting with the dear ones she was never to meet again, but it was an April shower succeeded by smiles. Each outburst of weeping was of shorter duration, and the sunny intervals between them were longer, till in a few days Grace was her bright self again. The excitement of the journey was so overwhelming as to swallow up every other feeling.

We reached our home one November afternoon, as the setting sun looked out through a rift in the clouds, and his level beams lighted up every casement with a red glow. As we drove up the leafless avenue, heavy drops fell from the bare boughs overhead, and Grace, clinging to my arm, said in a frightened whisper: "Oh Humphrey, that light in the window is not like sunshine! It looks as if your old house was on fire!" and raising my eyes I caught for one moment the full effect of the illusion. But, the sun sinking into his bed of cloud, the red glow faded from the windows and left them dark and dim. "Welcome, my darling, to your English home," I said, and I took my little wife by the hand and led her up the wide oak staircase; and before we sat down to our evening meal I had taken her over the house from garret to basement, preceding her, candle in hand, through the darkening rooms.

She expressed unbounded admiration for the house and its furniture, but the old family portraits and pictures excited her utmost enthusiasm, for Grace had never seen anything more venerable or older than her grandparents and the log house in which she was born. When her raptures had toned down sufficiently to allow her to eat a little, and we were seated at supper in the oak parlour, my little wife suddenly said, "Humphrey, there ought to be a ghost in a house like this."

"Why should there be?" I asked, while I smiled at her extreme gravity.

"Because so many generations of men and women cannot have been born and died in this house without leaving some trace of themselves for us who come after." And I saw that works of fiction had penetrated into the far west, for Grace had certainly been reading romances.

"I object to talking about ghosts at supper," I said. "Breakfast is the best time for such conversation, and not a word should be uttered on the subject later than twelve o'clock at noon;" and I rose, and taking one of the candles with me, and holding it so as to throw the light on a dark painting over the mantelshelf, I asked, "Do you know who that is?"

My little wife looked earnestly at the portrait, with her head inclined dubiously, and with a puzzled expression of face.

"I am not surprised that you do not know who that dark, sinister-looking man is, for the backwoods of America are not hung with portraits of Charles the Second. Yes, that is King Charles; and the melancholy cast of his features must be merely an inherited expression—certainly nothing in his nature answered to it—for he passed through grief and tragedy with a light heart. He once spent a night in this very house; we have the tradition of his visit, with many quaint details, preserved to this day."

"Oh how wonderful to think of it!" said Grace eagerly. "And would the king sup in this very room where you and I are now?"

"Yes, in this very room, and would you like to know what he had for supper?"

"No, that is nor the kind of thing that makes me curious. I want to know how the king looked, how he was dressed, and in which of those solemn-looking old bedrooms upstairs he slept. No doubt you still have the bed the king slept in?"

"No," I replied with decision. "That I am sure we have not."

"Then tomorrow, Humphrey, you will show me the room the king slept in, and the bed I can imagine for myself."

The bed she could imagine for herself! My little wife did not know what she was talking about. The next day the event occurred which might have been expected. I was walking in the garden, when Grace came to me, and slipping her hand through my harm, drew me towards the porch.

"You see that large window," she said, pointing towards it as she spoke. "That is the one I admired so much in the picture of the house. I have looked out of every window but that, and I fancy the room must be locked, for I cannot open it, so I have fetched you to unlock it for me."

I walked in silence by her side while she led me into the house and upstairs to the door of the hated room, talking with so much animation herself that she did nor notice that I had not spoken a word.

"This is the room," she said gaily, and she turned the latch of the door to and fro, saying as she did so, "You see it is locked."

"I know it is," I said sullenly.

"Then fetch the key and open it." Grace gave the door handle a little impetuous shake.

"My dearest, don't ask me again to open that door, for I shall not do it."

"Not do what I ask you to do? How cruel of you!" And her eyes filled with tears.

I knew that my young wife thought me brutal, but I could only say, "Anything else in my power I will do for you, only this one thing, this one little thing, I beg you will not ask me to do."

"If you admit that it is such a very small thing, there can be no reason why you should refuse to grant me such a trivial request," persisted Grace. "When I ask you simply to unlock a door in your own house, and you refuse to do it, I can only think that you do not love me, or else that there is some horrid mystery about the room that you wish to keep hidden from me." And she wiped away a hasty tear, that proceeded rather from indignation than from grief.

"My dear Grace, do not let us be tragic about nothing. There is no secret connected with this room that I have ever heard of, and I love you so much that I cannot bear to see you troubling yourself with absurd imaginations. The fact is this. I have a feeling—call it superstition, what you will—but I have a feeling that would make it very painful to me to open this door and take you into the room. And what pleasure could there be in seeing a bare, unfurnished room, precisely like any other empty room?"

"But I should set about furnishing it at once."

"Let us come away," I said, gently removing her dear, obstinate hand from the lock. "I repeat, I have a feeling about that room that would prevent my ever being happy in it." And, I added lightly, "Don't let my Eve spoil our paradise by longing after the forbidden fruit."

But Grace said quickly, "It was not Adam who forbade Eve to eat of the fruit. If it had been, I can't see that there would have been any great harm in disobeying him." And we said no more about the locked door, but a cloud had come between us, and the unalloyed sweetness of our first happiness was lost.

One day, a few weeks after this folly, when I was beginning to hope that my little wife had forgotten her curiosity, I saw from her constrained and uneasy manner that something had happened to disturb her.

"My dear Grace, you certainly are not happy this morning—will you not tell me what ails you?" I asked.

Her voice trembled and her face flushed as she replied. "Humphrey, I did not think you could tell me an untruth."

"My child, what do you mean? We are playing at cross purposes. Be so good as to explain your meaning, that we may not misunderstand each other for a moment."

"You told me that the big bedroom you keep locked was empty."

"So it is," I said, growing impatient at this childish scene, "but what is the untruth I have told you?"

"Why, the room is not empty. I can prove what I say."

"The room not empty! Nonsense! I keep the key, and none but myself has entered it these two years."

"How can you persist in such an untruth, Humphrey? I am not ashamed to confess that I looked through the keyhole—I wonder I did not do it before—and I saw in the middle of the room, between the door and the window, an enormous old bed. I could only see the two foot-posts, but they went up to the ceiling, and the footboard was high and richly carved, and the curtains a gloomy, dark green. So you have deceived me about the room, and I am afraid there is some secret connected with it that you dare not tell me. What ails you, Humphrey?"

And my wife rose with a terrified exclamation, for I thought I was fainting, and all the life seemed to have gone out of the air.

"Grace," I said, when I had shaken off the sense of oppression, "let us go at once to that unlucky room, and settle this preposterous dispute. You say that the room has furniture in it—I say that it is empty. We will see which of us is right, and then we will never mention the subject again." I asked my wife to come with me and assure herself that the room was, as I said, absolutely bare and unfurnished. My hand shook as I turned the key, and, flinging the door open till it strained on its hinges, we entered the room together.

Grace shrank back with a low cry, and covered her face with her hands.

"Where is it gone to, the great bed that I saw standing on this very spot? I cannot have been deceived. Oh Humphrey! Why

do you play me such cruel tricks? You terrify me."

"My little wife," I said, assuming an air of cheerfulness I was far from feeling, "this comes of what I must call your overweening curiosity. If my dear girl bad been content to let me keep this door locked, she would not have grown so curious that her little brain is almost turned, and she has taken to seeing housewifely spectral illusions of domestic furniture. Depend upon it, what you think you saw was nothing but the creature of your own imagination, that has dwelt so long on the idea of furnishing the room that you have only to peep through the keyhole, and, hey, presto! The thing is done, and beds and tables start forward at your bidding. But henceforward you can enter the room as often as you like, only we will not live in it, and I will not have it furnished."

This appeared to satisfy Grace, and though I could not fully persuade her that the great bed she had seen when she peeped through the keyhole was an illusion begotten of curiosity and a lively imagination, yet with the door of the room unlocked, she felt that she had some control over any tricks I might play her in the future.

I was deeply disturbed by what she had told me. I had not breathed a word to my wife about the destruction of the ancestral bed. Mrs Barrett was dead before we were married, and I had changed my servants since her death, and, as we saw nothing of our neighbours, Grace could not have heard from anyone of the ghastly old bed, which nevertheless she had accurately described to me.

I could never tell her the truth now. It would shake her nerves, and impress her with the idea that there was something weird about the house. I wished I had not destroyed the old bed. Better far that she should have known the gloomy reality than behold a presentment of it that was neither an embodiment of memory nor a vivid picturing of it from imagination. I tried if I could summon up a like hallucination, but in vain. Though my memory of the ancient bed was perfect, and every detail stamped on my mind, never could I call it up before my external vision, however earnestly I tried to do so.

Grace completely regained her accustomed cheerfulness, and in the spring was busy making a thousand little preparations for the expected arrival of an infant, which was to surpass any yet born into this world. I could hardly believe the gentle obstinacy of my wife, when, after all I had said about the empty room, she asked one day if she might not make it into a nursery.

"Do you not remember, dear, that I said we would not furnish that room?" I said.

"Oh, of course, not furnish it; a nursery needs no furniture; but it is much the most cheerful and sunny room in the house."

And again I had to appear inhuman and refuse my little wife a trivial request.

One morning as I sat in my room busy with my accounts, Grace came to tell me that she was going to drive to the county town, some eight miles distant, for a round of shopping, such as her soul loved. I said that if she would wait till the next day I should be able to take her myself, but she tapped the barometer on the wall, that had stood for some time at "set fair," and assured me it would rain tomorrow, and that she must avail herself of the fine weather today. So away drove my self-willed darling, nodding a gay farewell as the carriage drove away from the house.

Grace returned late in the afternoon in the best of spirits, bringing with her an enormous package such as none that a country woman, or one, like my little wife, from the far west, would dream of bringing with her in an open carriage. It must have broken the coachman's heart to drive with it through the streets of the county town.

"What in the name of wonder have you brought home with you?" I asked.

"Ah!" she said, laughing, "it is a trial for your curiosity now! Anything else you may ask me I will tell you, only I cannot let you know anything about this mysterious package."

"Then have it putout of sight," I said, "or depend upon it I shall find some hole in the wrapper to peep through. You ought to know what a devouring passion curiosity is."

As the unwieldy bundle was carried upstairs, its cover slipped aside and revealed a pair of black oak rockers. But I said nothing; Grace should tell me her little secret in her own way, and at her own time.

We thought ourselves the happiest creatures in the world when our little son Heneage was born. The gloom that brooded over the house from the death of many generations was lessened by the joy of birth, and my young son's life was like the sprouting acorn that sends up its vigorous shoot through the earth, fed by the fallen leaves of a hundred autumns. On the third day of our happiness my wife sent for me, and told me she had a very pretty surprise for me.

"I can tell you all about the big mysterious package now. It was a beautiful old-fashioned cradle that I bought in Carlyon from a man called Gillam, who keeps an old furniture shop here. I fell in love with it at once, for I knew how well it would suit this house with its old oak. Gillam said he could swear it was old work; in fact, he said it was originally part of a fine old bedstead a poor mad gentleman in the neighbourhood actually destroyed in a fit of frenzy, but he was lucky enough to secure a portion of the wreck, and made it up into that cradle, and baby looks lovely in it. I'm afraid I gave a great deal of money for it, but one does not meet with such a beautiful thing every day." And the nurse removed a screen from before the cradle, that its beauties might burst upon me suddenly and with the more effect.

Cold drops stood on my brow as I recognised, in the high sides and head of the cradle, the carving of ivy branches and berries I had so madly given Gillam when I destroyed the old bed.

"I thought you would have been so pleased," said Grace, disappointed by my silence as I stood spellbound, my eyes following every line of the hatred carving. "I thought you would have been so pleased to see baby in a cradle really worthy of him."

But I could not speak; I was oppressed by a sense of coming doom.

"It is very unkind of you," said Grace. "I had prepared a pretty surprise for you, and instead of being pleased, you stand and sigh and look as if you saw a ghost. Nurse, take baby out of his lovely cradle; we must get him a common wicker thing to lie in instead!" And the nurse did as her mistress bade her, and lifted little Heneage from his cradle of death, for while we talked the child had slept his feeble life away.

I have no memory of what happened day by day during the few weeks following. It was my one consuming fear that my wife too should die. Six weeks after our child's death I carried her downstairs, and this was the only progress made cowards recovery. She remained at the same stage of convalescence, made wayward by grief, with shattered nerves, and so weak in mind and body that I dared not thwart her in anything. As the dim, sunless days of autumn drew on, my little wife said to me as though we had never spoken on the subject before, "I want the big empty room furnished for my sitting room, Humphrey. I shall have a little sunshine there sometimes to cheer me in your dismal English winter, and it will amuse me to furnish it."

As I looked at her white wishful face, I felt that nothing mattered to me now, and I said, "Do exactly as you like, dear, in everything," and she was too listless to thank me.

But the work of transforming the sombre room into a bright boudoir proceeded rapidly, for Grace said with a shudder, "I will have no more old oak furniture."

My little wife always went to extremes, and now, in her antipathy to old oak, she filled the room with tawdry chips of furniture, chairs made of gilded matchsticks tied together with ribbons, that must sink into feeble ruins if a cat so much as jumped on them.

I entered into all her little fancies, and feigned excessive admiration of each fresh idea she had on the subject of decoration. I did her bidding, even to placing her couch on the very spot where the hated bed had stood. Thus was my resistance broken down, and I, who three years ago had tried by sheer physical force to thwart destiny, was now unconsciously working to bring about its fulfilment. It did not tarry long.

One gloomy November afternoon, Grace lay on her couch covered with soft shawls, and the window curtains were drawn back to give as much light as possible. The glow of the setting sun illuminated the room, and lent a more living hue to the grey pallor of her face.

"How like the day when I first came to Walford Grange" she said. "The sun is setting with the same fiery light. Do go into the garden, Humphrey, and see if the windows are aglow with red light as they were then." And I left her to do as she asked me.

Seen from the garden, the house looked precisely as it had done on the day of our homecoming. From garret to basement every window glowed red in the light of the setting sun, as though from fire within. Everything that my eyes rested on was as it had been a year ago. Grace and I only were changed—changed in ourselves and changed to each other. I felt impatient of the changeless aspect of nature and of inanimate things around me, and I entered the house, now dark in contrast with the twilight without, and returned to my wife's room with a heavy heart.

"The house looks as it did when you first saw it," I said. 'Till the sun sank behind the hill, the windows were lighted up with the same strange effect of fire that you noticed a year ago," and I threw a fresh log on the embers as I spoke, sending a bright train of sparks up the wide chimney. "Shall I light the candles?" I asked, turning towards my wife's couch. "The room is growing dark." But there was no reply. I was speaking to the dead.

In vain I had baulked the old bed of its prey, for there on the very spot where it had stood for three centuries and generations of my ancestors had died, the wife of the last of the Walfords lay dead.

I buried my sweet Grace by our little son, and on the night of the funeral, alone in my desolate home, I conceived the idea of freeing myself forever from the horror of darkness that had fallen on Walford

Grange. I sent every servant away. I would have the house and my sorrow to myself.

When I was assured that I was alone in the house, I went rapidly from room to room in a strange exultation, speaking aloud and flinging open doors and windows till the cold night air rushed through chambers and passages, and curtains and hangings flapped in the wind.

"When I destroyed the old bed of death," I said, "I thought to restore joy and brightness to Walford Grange. But I should have destroyed not it alone, but the room in which it stood, and the very house of which it formed a part. Never more shall man dwell in this house glutted with death. Never more shall the voice of the bride and bridegroom be heard in its chambers, or footsteps of children be heard on its stairs. Never more shall fire subdued to harmless household use be kindled on its hearth, but fire untamed in its ferocity shall devour the accursed pile." And I seized the burning log from the hearth and threw it on the couch where Grace had died.

Carrying a lighted brand, I sped from room to room of the doomed house, leaving in each a fiery token of my presence, and then, descending the wide staircase, where flickering shadows were cast from every open door, and the silence was broken by the crackling sound of flames, I let myself out into the darkness, closing the heavy door behind me with a crash.

On through the cold damp air I ran, the moon through a rift in the clouds guiding me by her fitful light, till, drawing her shroud around her, she left me again in darkness. Not once did I rum to right or left or look behind me till I had gained the summit of the hills that bounded the valley. Then I stood and turned to take a last look at the home of my fathers. Just then the moon, issuing forth in cold splendour from her bed of cloud, shed a solemn lustre far and wide. And I saw for the last time the house of my birth, the cradle and grave of my race, and every window from basement to garret glowed with fire, no mere reflected glare, but red from the raging fire within, and keen flames darted from the casement of the room above the porch.

I stood long to watch the fire of my own kindling, till when a sudden burst of light and leaping splendour of flame showed me that the gabled roof had fallen in, I shouted, took off my hat, and waved a last farewell to Walford Grange.

LOUISA BALDWIN (1845–1925) was a British novelist and short story writer best known for works such as *The Shadow on the Blind and Other Ghost Stories* (1895) and several novels including *A Martyr to Mammon* and *The Story of a Marriage*. She was the mother of British Prime Minister Stanley Baldwin.

SETH'S COMICS AND drawings have appeared in the *New York Times*, the *New Yorker*, the *Globe and Mail*, and countless other publications.

His graphic novel *Clyde Fans* won the prestigious Festival d'Angoulême's Prix Spécial du Jury.

He lives in Guelph, Ontario, with his wife, Tania, in an old house he has named "Inkwell's End."

Publisher's Note: "The Weird of the Walfords" was first published in *The Shadow on the Blind and Other Ghost Stories* (J. M. Dent & Co., 1889)

Library and Archives Canada Cataloguing in Publication

Title: The weird of the Walfords / Louisa Baldwin ; a ghost story for Christmas, designed & decorated by Seth.
Names: Baldwin, Louisa, 1845–1925, author.
Seth, 1962– illustrator.
Description: Series statement: Seth's Christmas ghost stories
Identifiers: Canadiana 20260197955
ISBN 9781771967457 (softcover)
Subjects: LCGFT: Ghost stories. | LCGFT: Christmas fiction.
LCGFT: Short stories.
Classification: LCC PS1059.B48 W45 2026 | DDC 813/.8—dc23

Readied for the press by Daniel Wells
Illustrated and designed by Seth
Copyedited by Ashley Van Elswyk
Typeset by Ingrid Paulson

PRINTED AND BOUND IN CANADA